Painted Skies

To my parents, Florence and Dale Herman, for inspiring me with their love of books.

Published by Inhabit Media Inc. • www.inhabitmedia.com

Inhabit Media Inc. (Iqaluit), P.O. Box 11125, Iqaluit, Nunavut, X0A 1H0
(Toronto), 191 Eglinton Avenue East, Suite 301, Toronto, Ontario, M4P 1K1

Editors: Neil Christopher and Louise Flaherty
Art director: Danny Christopher

Originally published in hardcover May 2015.

We acknowledge the financial support of the Government of Canada through the Department of Canadian Heritage Canada Book Fund.

We acknowledge the support of the Canada Council for the Arts for our publishing program.

Printed in Canada

Library and Archives Canada Cataloguing in Publication

Mallory, Carolyn, author
    Painted skies / by Carolyn Mallory ; illustrated by Amei Zhao.

Previously published: 2015.
ISBN 978-1-77227-219-2 (softcover)

    I. Zhao, Amei, 1985-, illustrator II. Title.

PS8626.A453P33 2018   jC813'.6   C2018-902855-6

Painted Skies

by Carolyn Mallory • illustrated by Amei Zhao

INHABIT
MEDIA

Leslie leapt off the steps, all arms and legs like a young caribou trying to keep up with the herd. *Whump!* The snow was hard packed, with only a light layer of fluff. Oolipika landed beside her, laughing. The girls lay on their backs, their breath forming small, frosty clouds.

They swept their arms and legs up and down as if they were ptarmigans trying to get off the ground and fly away.

"I didn't think there would be so much snow here in October," Leslie said. "I'm glad my mom bought me new winter clothes before we moved."

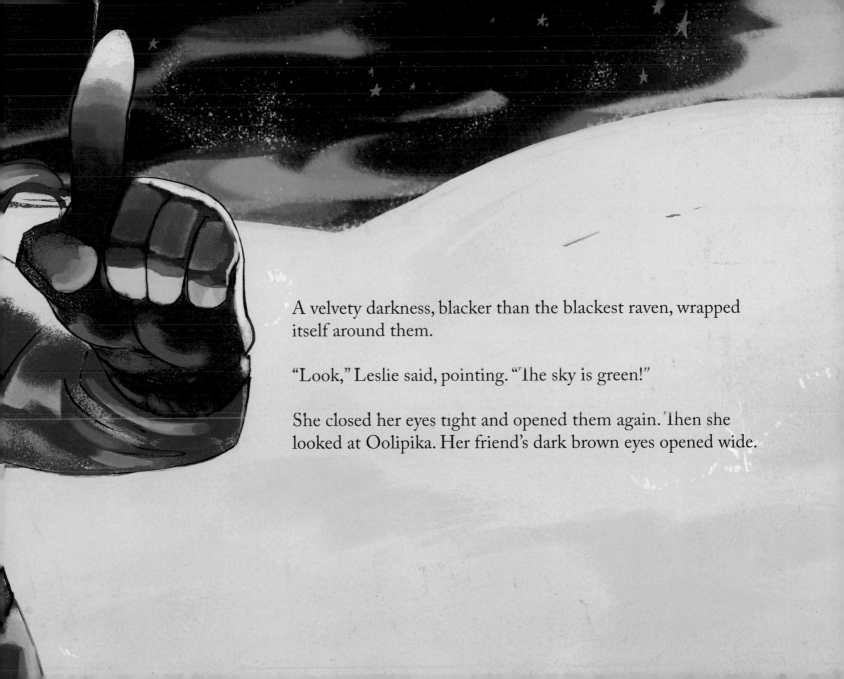

A velvety darkness, blacker than the blackest raven, wrapped itself around them.

"Look," Leslie said, pointing. "The sky is green!"

She closed her eyes tight and opened them again. Then she looked at Oolipika. Her friend's dark brown eyes opened wide.

Holding hands, the girls rose. Pink swirls now flashed with the lime green. Leslie moved closer to Oolipika.

Huge ribbons waved in the wind. Leslie shivered. The colours consumed more of the sky and glided closer like a silent snowy owl.

When Leslie was afraid, her mother had taught her to whistle. Squeezing Oolipika's hand, Leslie took a deep breath, pursed her lips, and started to blow.

"Stop whistling," Oolipika said. "They'll hear you." She took off her mitts and quickly moved the fingernails of one hand back and forth across the fingernails of her other hand, making a clicking noise.

"What will hear me?" Leslie asked.

Oolipika kept rhythmically moving one set of fingernails over the other.

Leslie inched steadily back to the house with Oolipika behind her. *If we move slowly*, she thought, *whatever's in the sky won't notice us.*

The stars twinkled through the green and pink silky sheet that rippled overhead. Leslie felt her heart beat a little faster. Could the sky-colours hear her? Would they get close enough to touch her?

"Spirits?" Leslie whispered to her friend.

Oolipika nodded her head. "*Anirniit*—spirits," she said.

Leslie held her breath and stared as the streaks of colour changed, painted more of the sky, and drifted closer.

"Should we run back to the house?" Leslie whispered to Oolipika.

"We don't have to be afraid, as long as you don't whistle again," Oolipika said.

"What kind of spirits are they?"

"*Aqsarniit* are what we call them, northern lights."

"Lights?" Leslie asked. "Not spirits?"

"Look closely," said Oolipika. "Do you see how all the long threads of light follow one after the other? Those are people running. That's what my grandma says."

"Oh," Leslie said, squinting her eyes. "Wow," she whispered. "I can see them."

"These lights are our anirniit, the spirits of our great-grandparents or friends that have died. They are playing a game with a ball, kind of like soccer," Oolipika said.

"My grandmother told me that if you whistle, the lights will come closer and the ball might hit you on the head. Because these spirits are very strong, they use a big, old walrus skull for a ball. Nobody wants to get hit by that ball! If you make clicking sounds with your fingernails, the spirits know to stay away."

Leslie looked up at the sky and smiled as she took off
her mittens and clicked her fingernails.

"They're beautiful," she said.

Sometimes green, sometimes red,
the night sky dances.
Stars peek through satin pink with
a wink and a flicker.
A wisp of yellow gauze
as the sky
breathes with light.
Splashes of purple and silver-grey,
a sail, a sheet, a streak—
with one great gust, gone.

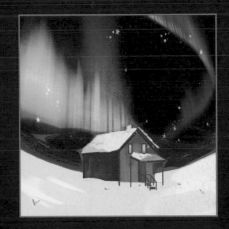

What Are Northern Lights?

Northern lights—aqsarniit in Inuktitut, or *aurora borealis*, as they are also called—are coloured lights that illuminate the night sky if the conditions are right.

Auroras are caused by high-speed particles from the sun striking the gases in the atmosphere. The earth is a giant magnet, which attracts these particles from the sun to its magnetic poles (north and south). The gases glow as a result of being hit by the particles. Since the particles are moving, it looks like lights are dancing across the sky.

Northern lights cannot be viewed from everywhere. The farther north you go in North America, the more likely you are to see these lights. You can also see them in northern Europe. Your best chance of seeing northern lights is on a clear, moonless night around midnight.